MAX VELTHUIJS

Little Man Finds a Home

North-South Books
New York   London   Toronto   Melbourne

There was once a tiny little man
who lived in an old cardboard shoe box.
He was happy there.

One day it began to rain.
Little Man was pleased.
"The rain will be good for my garden,"
he said.

But it rained for three days and three nights.
That was too much for the shoe box.
It was soaked with water
and fell down.

Little Man packed all his things
in a bundle and hurried away.
He stopped under a large tree
to get out of the rain.

A bird called down to him:
"Come up and join us.
It's dry up here and we're
having lots of fun."

Little Man climbed the tree but then...

...he fell down.
"Oh well," he said, "I'm not a bird.
I'd better stay on the ground."

Meanwhile the rain had stopped.
The sun made him warm and dry again.
"Now I can take my time to find a new house,"
he said to himself.

When night fell he still hadn't found a house.
So he lay down on the ground
and went to sleep with only
the sky for a roof over his head.

The next morning Little Man met a frog.
"Hello, Little Man!
I know where there's a good home for you,"
said the frog.
He led him to an empty jar.

It was a very fine house.
You could see through all the walls.
And it was waterproof.
But after an hour in the jar
Little Man felt much too hot.

He went on looking. Then he found a coffee pot
behind a tuft of grass.
"That would make a nice house," he thought.

But suddenly wasps came swarming out
of the spout.
"Go away," they buzzed. "This is our house."

Little Man ran away as fast as he could.

A little later he met a rabbit.
"Come and live with us, Little Man,"
said the rabbit.
"It's cozy in our house,
and there's plenty of room."

Little Man liked living with the rabbits.
Every evening they played chess
and drank carrot juice.

But one morning thirteen baby rabbits suddenly arrived
and there was no room for Little Man anymore.
He thanked the rabbits warmly for their kindness
and went on his way.

Outside he met a snail.
"How nice," he thought,
"to carry your home with you wherever you go."

Soon after that he met a Little Woman picking apples.
"Can I help you?" he asked, and the Little Woman said,
"Yes, please."

When all the apples were picked
Little Man carried the basket
and Little Woman carried his bundle.

In Little Woman's house they made
a big bowl of soup for their supper.
And Little Man decided to stay forever.

The next Sunday they invited all the
animals to a party.

There was a big feast with lots of good things
to eat. Only one of the animals was missing – the snail.

She was so slow that she only arrived
after all the others had gone home.
Luckily, Little Man and Little Woman
had saved a bowl of salad
especially for her.

Copyright © 1983 Nord-Süd Verlag, Mönchaltorf, Switzerland
First published in Switzerland under the title Klein-Mannchen hat kein Haus
English text copyright © 1983 Abelard-Schuman Ltd
Copyright English language edition under the imprint
North-South Books © 1985 Rada Matija AG, Staefa, Switzerland

First published in Great Britain in 1983
under the imprint Abelard/North-South by Abelard-
Schuman Ltd and reprinted in 1985 by North-South Books,
an imprint of Rada Matija AG.
First published in the United States, Australia and New
Zealand in 1985 by North-South Books, an imprint of
Rada Matija AG.

Distributed in the United States by
Holt, Rinehart and Winston, 383 Madison Avenue,
New York, New York, 10017.
Library of Congress Cataloging in Publication Data

Velthuijs, Max, 1923 –
   Little man finds a home.

   Translation of: Klein-Mannchen hat kein Haus.
   Summary: Little man loses the cardboard box in which
he has been living and goes out among the animals of the
world to find a new home.
   1. Children's stories, German – Swiss Authors.
   [1. Dwellings – Fiction. 2. Animals – Fiction] I. Title.
PZ7.V51   1985   [E]   85-7247

ISBN 0-03-005734-5

Distributed in Great Britain by
Blackie and Son Ltd, Furnival House, 14—18 High Holborn,
London WC1V 6BX.
British Library Cataloguing in Publication Data

Lanning, Rosemary
   Little man finds a home.
   I. Title   II. Velthuijs, Max. Klein
   Mannchen hat kein Haus
   823'.914[J]   PZ7

ISBN 0-200-72840-7

Distributed in Australia and New Zealand by
Buttercup Books Pty. Ltd., Melbourne.
ISBN 0 949447 07 2

Printed in Germany